天线宝宝
Teletubbies ™
迪西和花带

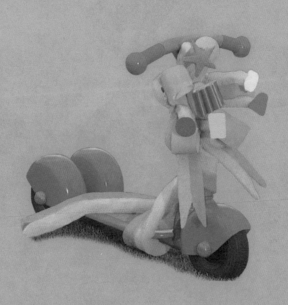

童趣出版有限公司编译　　　人民邮电出版社出版

一天，在天线宝宝乐园里，有个东西从远方出现了。
One day in Teletubbyland, something
appeared from far away.

多漂亮的
东西啊！

它是一条花带。
It was a decoration.

花带装饰在树上。
The decoration decorated the tree.

后来，花带消失了。
Then, the decoration
disappeared.

叮！

花带装饰在房子上。
The decoration decorated the house.

叮！

后来，花带消失了。
Then, the decoration
disappeared.

花带装饰在小波的滑板车上。
The decoration decorated Po's scooter.

多漂亮啊！
How decorative!

后来，花带
消失了。
Then, the
decoration
disappeared.

花带装饰在丁丁的包上。
The decoration decorated Tinky Winky's bag.

多漂亮啊!
How decorative!

后来，花带消失了。
Then, the decoration disappeared.

花带装饰在拉拉的球上。
The decoration decorated Laa-Laa's ball.

噢！
看！
花带！

多漂亮啊！
How decorative!

多漂亮啊！

迪西来了。
Along came Dipsy.

拉拉给迪西看花带。
Laa-Laa showed Dipsy the decoration.

后来，花带消失了。
Then, the decoration disappeared.

看！花饰在瓶里了下
Look at that! The decoration had decorated itself!

花带跑哪儿去了?
Where had the
decoration gone?

花带!
花带!

花带!

看啊！花带装饰在迪西身上！
Look at that! The decoration had decorated Dipsy!

花带装饰在
迪西身上！

喔，不！

快跑！

快跑！

甩啊甩！
甩啊甩！

甩啊甩！
甩啊甩！

后来，花带消失了。
And then the decoration disappeared.

天线宝宝相亲相爱！
Teletubbies love each other very much.

抱抱！

1）花带装饰在哪个天线宝宝的滑板车上了？

2）花带装饰在哪个天线宝宝的包上了？

3）花带装饰在哪个天线宝宝身上了？

小羊羔

童趣出版有限公司编译　　　人民邮电出版社出版

一天，在天线宝宝乐园里，一个东西在远方出现了。

One day in Teletubbyland, something appeared from far away.

噢！

那是什么？

是一只小羊羔。
It was a little lamb.

拉拉以为小羊羔很伤心。
Laa-Laa thought the little lamb was sad...

于是，拉拉跳了一小段舞想让小羊羔高兴起来。
so Laa-Laa did a little dance to make
the little lamb happy.

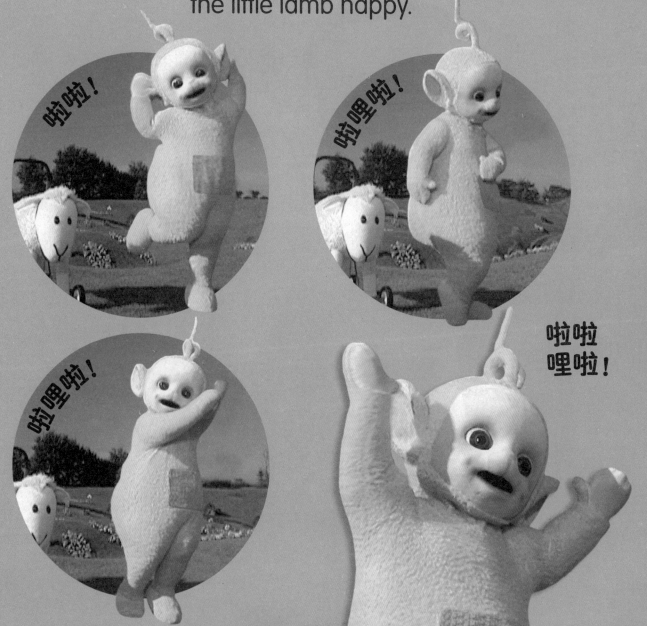

可小羊羔还是很伤心。
But the little lamb was still sad.

丁丁过来了。
Along came Tinky Winky.

丁丁觉得小羊羔不高兴
是因为它想到花朵旁边去。
Tinky Winky thought the little lamb was sad
because it wanted to be by the flowers.

花朵在那边！
There.

到那儿去！

可小羊羔还是很伤心。
But the little lamb was still sad.

迪西过来了。
Along came Dipsy.

你好，迪西！ 你好，拉拉！ 你好，丁丁！

噢！那是什么？

一只小羊羔！唉！

咩……咩……咩！

迪西觉得小羊羔不高兴
是因为它想戴他的帽子。
Dipsy thought the little lamb was sad
because it wanted to wear his hat.

小羊羔
戴帽子！

帽子在这儿。
There.

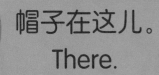

戴上吧！

可小羊羔还是很伤心。
But the little lamb was still sad.

小波过来了。
Along came Po.

小波觉得小羊羔不高兴是因为
它想玩她的滑板车。
Po thought the little lamb was sad because
it wanted to ride her scooter.

小羊羔
玩滑板车！

滑板车在这儿。
There.

玩吧！

但小羊羔还是很伤心。
But the little lamb was still sad.

咩……咩……咩！

嗐！

后来，天线宝宝们听到一个声音。
Then the Teletubbies heard a noise.

那是另一只小羊羔!
It was another little lamb!

两只小羊羔好高兴啊！
The little lambs were HAPPY!

高兴的小羊羔！
Happy lambs!

天线宝宝相亲相爱。
Teletubbies love each other very much!

1）小羊羔是怎么叫的？

2）丁丁把小羊羔送到什么东西旁边去了？

3）这个故事里一共有几只小羊羔？

宝宝烤面包塔

童趣出版有限公司编译　　　人民邮电出版社出版

一天，在天线宝宝乐园里，
吃宝宝烤面包的时间到了。
One day in Teletubbyland,
it was time for tubby toast.

丁丁、迪西和拉拉坐在了宝宝座位上。
Tinky Winky, Dipsy and Laa-Laa
sat on the tubby seats...

小波去按宝宝烤面包机上的按钮。
...and Po pressed the button
on the tubby toaster.

一片宝宝烤面包从宝宝烤面包机里飞了出来……

A piece of tubby toast flew
out of the tubby toaster...

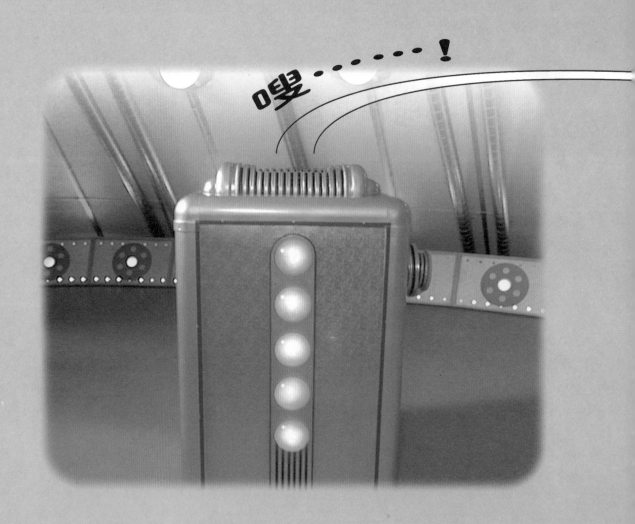

落到了宝宝桌的中央。
...and landed in the middle of the tubby table.

随后，**又一片**宝宝烤面包从宝宝烤面包机里飞了出来，
Then **another** piece of tubby toast
flew out of the tubby toaster

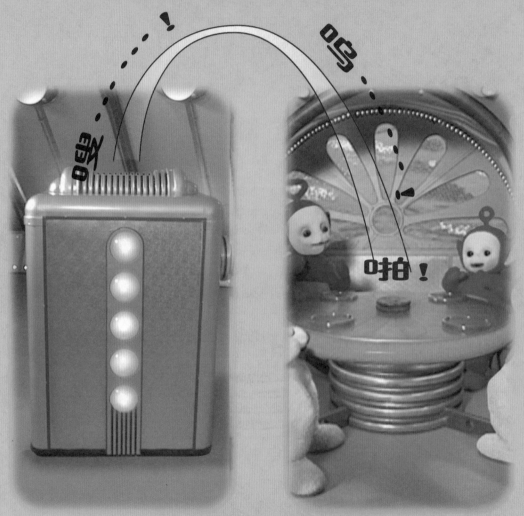

落到了宝宝桌的中央。
and landed in the middle of the tubby table.

然后，又一片……
Then another piece

一片又一片，一片又一片……
and another and another and another...

宝宝烤面包叠成了一座宝宝烤面包塔！
The tubby toaster had made
a tower of tubby toast!

拉拉想要一片宝宝烤面包。
Laa-Laa wanted a piece of tubby toast.

但她够不着。
But she couldn't reach.

拉拉够不着！

迪西想要一片宝宝烤面包。
Dipsy wanted a piece of tubby toast.

但他够不着。
But he couldn't reach.

丁丁想要一片宝宝烤面包。
Tinky Winky wanted a piece of tubby toast.

但他够不着。
But he couldn't reach.

丁丁够不着！

小波想要一片宝宝烤面包。
Po wanted a piece of tubby toast.

于是她拿了离她最近的一片。
So she took the nearest one.

宝宝烤面包塔开始晃来晃去，然后……
The tower of tubby toast wobbled and
wobbled, and then...

倒了!
... it FELL DOWN!

小波拿了一片宝宝烤面包。
Po had a piece of tubby toast...

现在**每个人**都有宝宝烤面包了。
...and now **everybody** could have tubby toast.
聪明的小波！
Clever Po!

每个人都有宝宝烤面包！

吧唧吧唧！

吧唧吧唧！

吸呀吸！

天线宝宝喜欢宝宝烤面包。
天线宝宝相亲相爱！
The Teletubbies love tubby toast.
And Teletubbies love each other very much!

1) 哪个宝宝去按烤面包机上的按钮？

2) 宝宝烤面包是什么形状的？

3) 宝宝烤面包都落到哪里了？